Fairy Ponies

Pony Princess

Zanna Davidson

Illustrated by Barbara Bongini

Meet the Ponies

Holly

Puck

Bluebell

Pony Queen

Princess Rosabel

Spray

Unicorn Prince

Izagard

Shadow

High Mountains

Izagard's House

Rainbow Mountain

Everlasting Rainbow

Summer Palace

Forever Flower Meadow

Rainbow Shore

Butterfly Valley

Silver Stream

Singing River

Meadows

Entrance from the Great Oak

N
W E
S

Contents

Chapter One   7

Chapter Two   18

Chapter Three   36

Chapter Four   44

Chapter Five   61

Chapter Six   71

Chapter Seven   83

Chapter Eight   89

Chapter One

Holly lay awake in her attic bedroom at Great-Aunt May's house, thinking about what an amazing summer vacation she was having. It was more exciting than she ever could have dreamed. Adventures with fairy ponies! She had been to their magical land, Pony Island, three times now. And tonight, she was ready for another adventure...

There was the sound of footsteps on the stairs and Great-Aunt May came into the room, her red hair tumbling over her shoulders, her long dress swishing as she walked. "Sweet dreams," she said to Holly, tucking her in. Then, blowing her a kiss goodnight, she went out, gently closing the door behind her.

Holly waited a minute or two, then crept out of bed. There was no sign of her great-aunt, so she padded down the stairs, through the back door and out into the starlit garden.

Ahead, she could see the old oak tree, its towering branches silhouetted against the sky. Holly ran down the lawn toward it, her bare feet silent on the soft grass. When she reached the tree, Holly glanced around to make sure no one was watching, then carefully slipped her fingers into a tiny bag of magic dust. The dust sparkled in her palm, full of the promise of magical adventure. Holly sprinkled it over herself, whispering the words of a spell the Pony Queen had taught her:

"Let me pass into the magic tree,
Where fairy ponies fly wild and free.
Show me the trail of sparkling light,
To Pony Island, shining bright."

There was a rush of wind and a tingling in her toes as Holly felt herself shrink down to fairy-size. Everything loomed above her, the grasses now as big as trees.

At last she was small enough to enter the secret tunnel in the oak tree that led straight to Pony Island.

Her heart fluttering with excitement, Holly set off down the tunnel, following the beam of light that stretched out before her. As she ran, she reached for the tiny silver bell she always wore around her neck, a gift from the Pony Queen. She rang the bell until its magical chime sounded through the tunnel, drifting out into Pony Island to let her best friend, Puck, know she was on her way.

At the end of the tunnel, the smooth oak pathway gave way to waving grasses and Holly ran out into a wildflower meadow. Puck was already waiting, his butterfly wings shimmering as he came bounding toward her.

"I'm so glad you're here!" he cried, his voice breathless with excitement. "The Pony

Queen has a special job for us!"

"What is it?" asked Holly, wrapping her arms around Puck's neck to give him a hug.

"I'm not sure yet," he replied. "But it's the annual Pony Island Costume Contest tonight, down in Butterfly Valley."

Holly swung herself onto Puck's back, loving the feel of his silky coat beneath her fingertips. "Maybe she's going to ask us to help! Oh, I can't wait to find out what our job is. Let's go!"

Puck flapped his wings and they soared into the air, gliding over meadows, winding rivers and wooded glades. Holly wondered if she'd ever get over the excitement of flying – the wind in her hair, the breathtaking views.

"What kind of costumes does everyone

make for the contest?" Holly asked.

"We use petals and feathers, leaves and dewdrops," Puck explained, "and make cloaks and headdresses and necklaces. Some ponies weave flowers into their manes and tails. The winner last year had an amazing cape made of lilies!"

"Can we enter the Costume Contest?"

"Of course we can!" Puck replied. "We just need to make our costumes. I've got some brilliant ideas."

Puck began telling Holly all about them, only stopping when the sparkling towers of the Summer Palace came into view. Its marble walls were covered in climbing roses, while the gardens bloomed with beautiful flowers.

Puck glided down onto the palace lawn,

where the Pony Queen was having tea, a young fairy pony at her side.

"Welcome," the queen said, in her lilting voice, her gossamer wings glimmering in the sunlight. "I have someone I'd like you both to meet."

She nodded toward the little pony, a beautiful palomino with patterned wings and a sparkling tiara resting on her shining mane.

"This is Princess Rosabel, my niece. She is visiting us from Waterfall Island, a magical land across the sea from Rainbow Shore."

Holly smiled warmly at the princess, who smiled back, rising gracefully from the grass and trotting over to greet them.

"It's a pleasure to meet you both," the princess said to Puck and Holly. "I'm so excited about making new friends on Pony Island."

"It is Princess Rosabel's first visit here," the Pony Queen went on, "and I have chosen you two to look after her. I know you'll make her feel welcome. Will you also help with her costume for the Costume Contest this evening?"

"Of course we will," said Puck, swelling with pride. He grinned at Princess Rosabel, who grinned back. "You've chosen the right team to take care of her, Your Majesty."

"Thank you," said the Pony Queen. She turned and kissed Princess Rosabel goodbye, before trotting back into the palace.

"Oh dear," said Princess Rosabel, her smile fading as soon as the Pony Queen had gone. "It looks like I'm stuck with you two."

Chapter Two

Puck and Holly exchanged glances as Princess Rosabel tossed her silken mane and stamped her painted hoofs. "Don't just stand there staring," she snapped. "You might as well be useful. You can cast a sewing spell, can't you? I want a costume and I want one now."

Puck's mouth hung open, as if he couldn't

believe what he was hearing. "You can't talk
to us like that!" he gasped.

"I don't see why not," snapped Princess
Rosabel. "It's not as if you're royal. And you
can't be that important if you've got a human
with you," she added, looking over at Holly
with disdain.

Holly could see Puck's face burning with anger and thought it might be best to change the subject. "I didn't know there were lands beyond Pony Island," she said gently. "In fact, I've never heard of Waterfall Island before."

"You've never heard of Waterfall Island?" repeated Princess Rosabel, shocked. "You obviously don't know very much about fairy ponies then. My island is the most beautiful of them all."

"Not everyone's heard of your island," said Puck huffily. "And how do you know it's the most beautiful, when you've never even been to Pony Island before?"

"Everyone knows," said Princess Rosabel.

"Oh really?" retorted Puck.

"I've got an idea!" said Holly quickly, seeing that Puck was about to launch into an argument. "Why don't we go on a tour of Pony Island, before we start thinking about our costumes? It might give us some inspiration."

"If I must," drawled Princess Rosabel. "At least it won't take long. I've heard it's much smaller than Waterfall Island."

"Prepare to be amazed," Puck replied. "Pony Island will be like nothing you've ever seen before."

Puck glanced back at Holly, rolling his eyes with a mischievous grin on his face. Holly quickly stifled a giggle. Then he fluttered his butterfly wings and they rose up into the air.

With a sigh, Princess Rosabel took off
behind them. Holly looked back to make sure
the princess could keep up with them, but she
quickly realized that Princess Rosabel was
just as strong a flier as Puck, her glittery
wings effortlessly cutting a swathe through
the summer air.

As they flew, Holly looked around her with

pleasure. Pony Island was at its most

beautiful in the early morning light, a hazy

mist cloaking the grass, petals unfurling after

a clear, cool night.

Puck pointed out all the most beautiful

spots on the island. They flew over the

Singing River, listening to the music it made

as it flowed, and passed by a peaceful glade,

its trees shimmering with magic. Beyond, they could just make out the shadow of the Dark Forest stretching away into the distance. They swooped down through the Forever Flower Meadow. Finally, Puck took them to Rainbow Shore, where the Everlasting Rainbow blazed across the sky. Even though she had seen it all before, Holly still felt dazzled by its beauty.

"Isn't it perfect?" she said, turning to Princess Rosabel.

Princess Rosabel yawned. "It's as I expected – nothing compared to Waterfall Island. Our golden beaches stretch for miles. But this is pretty enough in its own small way."

Holly gasped at the rudeness of her tone, while Puck snorted in anger. But Holly forced herself to remember that Princess Rosabel was their guest. "Let's head back to the palace," she suggested, before Puck could say anything. "It's probably time we started making our costumes for the Costume Contest."

"My costume must be the best," Princess Rosabel declared as they flew. "I'm determined to win."

They glided through the palace door, then trotted into the courtyard. *She must be impressed by this*, thought Holly, taking in the splashing fountains, and the twining branches that arched above their heads to form a vast, domed ceiling.

"Everything's just so small here," Princess Rosabel sighed. "Our palace at home is ten times the size." She tossed her head snootily. "I'm going to my bedroom now. I want you to start work on my costume immediately."

"I don't believe her," Puck whispered to Holly as they followed Princess Rosabel up the winding staircase to her room. "She's just boasting. I bet she's making it all up."

"Well, I wish she wouldn't…" Holly whispered back, before she was interrupted by a gasp of surprise.

Princess Rosabel had stopped in her tracks, gazing in wonder at a beautiful cloak that was hanging from a hook next to her bedroom window. It was made of dazzling feathers and flower petals, studded with shining jewels and shimmering with magic dust.

"Where did that come from?" she cried, moving forward as if in a daze.

"It's amazing," added Puck, trotting toward the cloak, suddenly desperate to touch it.

"It's mine!" snapped Princess Rosabel, barging past Puck to stand between him and the cloak. "Someone must have left it here for me," she added, greed flashing in her eyes. "My admirers are always doing things like that. I'll wear it to the Costume Contest, and then I'll be sure to win."

"Isn't it strange that someone just left it?"

said Holly, as drawn to the cloak as the others.

But before she could say anything more, Rosabel grabbed the cloak and flung it on. It fluttered through the air, landing gracefully over her back.

"You can't take it away from me," she said to Puck and Holly.

"We weren't going to," retorted Puck.

"You do look lovely in it," added Holly, trying to appease her, but she was puzzled by the hard, glittery expression in the princess's eyes.

"I do, don't I?" Rosabel agreed, twirling around so the cloak billowed out, its feathery fringes gliding through the air, its sparkle dust glinting in the sunlight. "I'll win the competition for sure now."

Puck snorted, clearly unimpressed. "Well, if you've got your costume, we'll go to the palace gardens and start making ours," he said. "See you later, Princess Rosabel."

But it was as if she hadn't heard him. Princess Rosabel stayed exactly where she was, gazing at herself in the mirror.

"To think I was so excited about our job for the Pony Queen," muttered Puck, as he and

Holly descended the stairs and went out into the palace gardens. "Princess Rosabel is almost as bad as Shadow. She's selfish, rude, hoity-toity—"

"No pony is as bad as Shadow," interrupted Holly. "Who else would be so wicked as to try to overthrow the Pony Queen? Princess Rosabel is just a bit…" Holly searched for the right word, "…spoiled."

"A *bit*?" cried Puck.

Holly could see he was working himself up into a temper. "Come on!" she said. "I'm not going to let her ruin our day. Let's design our costumes." She glanced around the palace gardens, looking for inspiration. "How about weaving these leaves together to make a headdress? And I think I'm going to try making bracelets and necklaces out of flowers."

They worked hard at their costumes, Puck roaming the gardens to find the largest, glossiest leaves, while Holly sat by the riverbank, threading together daisies, violets, buttercups and primroses, until she had made beautiful bracelets to wind up her arms and garlands to wear in her hair.

"I've finished!" cried Puck at last, cantering over to her, a proud smile on his face.

Holly had to try very hard not to laugh. Puck had bound some twigs together to make his headdress, then added leaves, and plonked it over his ears. It kept falling down though, covering his eyes like a helmet.

"What's so funny?" Puck asked, as Holly broke into giggles.

"Sorry," said Holly. "I, um, just wondered what you are, that's all."

"I'm a forest warrior," said Puck, "can't you tell?" He proudly tossed his head as he spoke, but that just made his headdress slide farther down his nose.

Holly giggled some more.

Puck suddenly caught sight of his reflection in the palace pond. "I look like a troll, don't I?" he chuckled.

"Yes," spluttered Holly, shaking with laughter.

But their laughter was interrupted by an imperious little voice. "There you are!"

Holly and Puck spun around to see Princess Rosabel standing behind them, still wearing her incredible cloak.

"I've just had an ingenious idea," she declared. "I need to sprinkle myself with dragonflower dust. Only then will my costume be complete."

"Dragonflower dust?" asked Holly.

"Yes, from the dragonflower plant. Its leaves are covered in a magical dust that will match my cloak perfectly. Then I'll sparkle everywhere."

As Princess Rosabel spoke, Holly noticed that her voice had taken on a strange, dreamlike quality.

"Well, you'll just have to do without it," said Puck. "The dragonflower only grows in the Dark Forest, and we can't go there. It's off limits."

"I don't care," said Princess Rosabel. "You

must escort me there immediately."

"We can't," said Puck. "The forest is full of dark magic and I'm not going there just to get you some dust."

Holly listened in surprise. It wasn't like Puck to turn down the chance to explore a part of Pony Island, even if it was off limits. He must have been really fed up with Princess Rosabel's orders.

"Fine!" snapped Princess Rosabel. "If you won't take me, I'll go by myself. I saw where it was on our tour of the island. Obviously, if anything happens to me, it'll be your fault." And with that, she kicked into the air, heading straight for the Dark Forest.

Chapter Three

Holly was filled with worry as she watched Princess Rosabel fly away. "Puck, we can't let her go alone," she said. "What if something does happen to her?"

"She's bluffing," said Puck scornfully. "There's no way that prissy little princess will go into the Dark Forest by herself."

"We don't know that for sure," Holly

pointed out. "I really think we should go after her."

"But I haven't finished making my costume," Puck complained. "And I'm hungry."

"We need to go now," said Holly. "Imagine if Princess Rosabel got lost, or worse..."

"How about a very quick lunch, then we go?" suggested Puck hopefully.

"Think of the Pony Queen," insisted Holly. "She gave us the job of looking after Rosabel. We can't let her down."

Puck sighed. "Okay. You're right. But I don't like the Dark Forest, and this is the last thing I'm doing for Princess Rosabel!"

As they soared away from the Summer Palace, Holly scanned the skies for any sign of the princess. At last they caught a glimpse of her just ahead, not far from where the gentle summer meadows ended, and the Dark Forest began.

"There she is!" cried Holly. "She's just at the edge of the forest."

Puck put on a new burst of speed to catch up with Rosabel, until the two ponies were flying neck and neck.

"Stop!" Holly called out to Rosabel. "Don't go in there...please!"

"You don't understand how dangerous it is," Puck added.

But the princess didn't even turn her head in acknowledgement – she just continued flying straight for the trees rising up ahead.

"We've got to do something!" cried Holly.

Puck flapped his wings furiously and darted in front of Princess Rosabel, trying to block her way, but she zigzagged past him without even a glance in their direction.

Panting for breath, Puck was forced to fly even faster to catch up with her.

By now they had reached the Dark Forest and, without warning, Princess Rosabel suddenly disappeared between the forbidding trees. "Uh-oh!" muttered Puck. He drew to a halt, hovering at the edge of the forest. "We can't go in there," he said, trying to catch his breath. "If I follow Rosabel, I'm putting you in danger as well."

Holly peered into the gloom ahead of them. The forest was very dark, and eerily silent. It felt almost as if the trees were watching them.

"We can't just leave her," Holly said. "We'll have to fly back to the Summer Palace immediately, and tell the Pony Queen what's happened."

"But I'm exhausted!" said Puck. "And I still haven't had my lunch."

"Puck!" said Holly warningly.

"I know, I know," said Puck. "We'll fly back. Just don't expect me to go at top speed."

"I just hope nothing happens to her in there,"

Holly worried as they flew away from the forest.

"It won't," said Puck. "Even really wicked ponies will stay far away from bossy Princess Rosabel, if they've got any sense."

But, despite what he said, Holly thought he sounded a little uneasy as they sped through the sky.

And as the topmost turrets of the Summer Palace came into view, Holly's heart plummeted – the palace was in uproar. Fairy ponies were flying around everywhere, anxious expressions on their faces, and troubled shouts filled the air.

Something was very wrong.

Chapter Four

The Pony Queen hurried over as soon as she
saw Puck and Holly canter into the courtyard.
"Something terrible has happened – a message
has just appeared from Shadow," she said. "One
of our Spell-Keepers, Snowdrop, is about to read
it. He says it's about Princess Rosabel... Go
on," she added, nodding to Snowdrop.

Snowdrop unfurled the message, which

hovered in the air on a parchment scroll.

"I'll read it aloud for everyone to hear," he said:

*Princess Rosabel is mine now.
I've kidnapped her and
she won't be coming back...
unless the Pony Queen gives
up her throne – to me. You
have until tomorrow morning
to make your decision. Make
the right one, or you will never
see Princess Rosabel again.*

*Shadow,
Lord of Darkness*

The Pony Queen paused for a moment before speaking, as if measuring her words carefully. "Shadow is a cold, calculating and evil pony and he has long wanted to take over Pony Island. We will not rest until we have Princess Rosabel back," she said. There was no tremor in her voice.

She turned to Puck and Holly. "I trusted you two. I thought you were looking after the princess. What happened?"

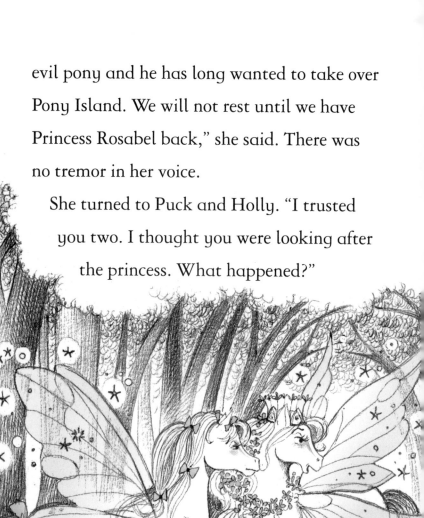

Puck explained as quickly as he could. The Pony Queen's trusted advisors, the Spell-Keepers, gathered around to listen, their eyes grave. Bluebell, Puck's mother, spoke first.

"You should never have let Princess Rosabel fly to the Dark Forest," she said sternly.

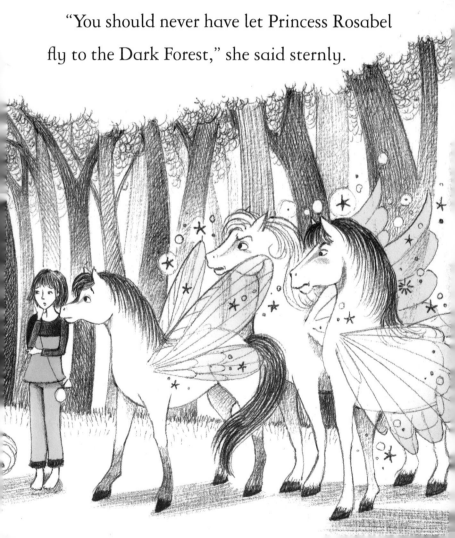

"You've let the Pony Queen down and put Rosabel in great danger."

Puck hung his head in shame.

"I'm so sorry," said Holly. "But I don't understand it. We did try to stop her. It was as if she was under some kind of enchantment," she went on, thinking of the hard glitter in Rosabel's eyes, the way she hadn't even stopped to listen to them.

"It's true," said Puck. "There really was nothing we could do to make her turn back."

Bluebell shook her head, still looking worried. "She was in your charge, Puck," she said.

"I feel terrible that we lost Rosabel," said Puck. "And I'm sorry we let you down, Your Majesty," he added, turning to the Pony

Queen. "Please, let us help—"

Bluebell cut him off with another shake of her head. "No. It's far too dangerous – only the Spell-Keepers can find her now. What are your orders?" she asked the Pony Queen.

"Spell-Keepers – I want you to fly to the Dark Forest and look for the princess and any sign of Shadow. I am going to send a message asking fairy ponies everywhere to be on the lookout for Rosabel. Her safety is the most important thing."

"We'll leave right away, Your Majesty," said Snowdrop. Holly watched the Spell-Keepers canter out of the courtyard before streaking into the sky, their wings a blur of motion.

Bluebell stayed behind a moment longer. "You're not to follow us to the Dark Forest,

Puck," she instructed. "And please, try to stay out of trouble. Promise?"

"I promise," Puck sighed, following his mother out of the courtyard and watching as she flew to join the other Spell-Keepers. He kicked the grass of the palace lawn in frustration.

"I suppose there's nothing for us to do now but wait here for news," he said glumly, turning back toward the Summer Palace.

"It wasn't your fault, Puck," said Holly, trying to comfort him. "We did try to stop Princess Rosabel."

"We should have tried harder," said Puck. "She might be the most stuck-up pony I've ever met, but I feel terrible that Shadow's taken her. If only there was something we could do."

Puck paused for a moment, and Holly could tell by his furrowed brow that he was thinking hard.

"Wait a minute!" he said at last, his eyes lighting up. "There is something we can do... Climb on my back, Holly. We're going to look for Princess Rosabel."

"Oh no we're not," said Holly, standing her ground. "We've already let the Pony Queen down. We can't disobey your mother as well."

"Who said we were going to the Dark Forest?" said Puck. "The Pony Queen has asked everyone to be on the lookout for Rosabel, and that's what we're going to do."

As soon as Holly was on his back, Puck flew hard and fast, his head lowered in determination, his ears flat against his head.

Holly had to bend all the way down as the wind whooshed over her back.

"Okay, so what's your plan?" she asked, as Puck began to head east across Pony Island.

"Shadow could have hidden Princess Rosabel anywhere on the island. And if there's one thing I'm excellent at, it's finding good hiding places. I want to check out all the ones I know."

"You never give up, do you?" said Holly, smiling down at him. But she felt relieved at

the thought of doing something to help.
"Where should we go first?"

"Let's try the woods at the bottom of the
High Mountains," suggested Puck.

He began by flying low over the treetops,
with Holly leaning over his side, scanning the
ground for a glimpse of Princess Rosabel.

"It's hard to see anything from up here,"
said Holly. "Do you think we should try
searching on foot?"

Puck nodded, swooping down into a little
clearing, his hoofs crashing to the mossy
ground.

"I used to come here with my friend,
Dandelion," Puck explained. "It was a great
place for hide-and-seek. Let's hope Shadow's
had the same idea."

But after an hour of searching, peering into hollowed-out trunks and between gnarled branches, there was still no sign of Rosabel.

"I don't think they came here," Puck said at last, scrambling out from another hollow tree. "It's time we moved on."

"How about the caves behind the Dancing Waterfall?" Holly suggested. "Shadow's hidden there before, remember?"

"Brilliant!" said Puck eagerly.

When they arrived at the little sandy shore
beside the waterfall, Holly slid from Puck's
back, shaking the spray from her hair. Then,
together, they crept into the caves. But there
was no sign of the princess anywhere.

"It's too dark," Puck complained. "We
won't be able to see Princess Rosabel, even if
she is here."

"Shh!" said Holly, holding Puck back.
"Let's just listen."

But the only sound was the distant roar of
the waterfall. Holly beckoned to Puck and they
emerged, dazed, into the sunlight once more.
"They're not in the caves," Holly said. "I'm sure
of it. And look," she added, "I can't see any

prints in the sand, besides our own."

"I can think of one more place to try," said Puck. "The abandoned huts beyond Pony Magic School. They're off limits, but I went there once as a dare," he added proudly.

Holly could tell Puck was growing tired as they flew on, past the thatched roof of Pony Magic School, with its jumps and playing fields dotting the ground below them, and on to the tumbledown huts.

"What happened to them?" Holly asked, taking in the holes in their roofs, the broken windows and rickety stairs.

"They used to be part of the school," Puck explained, "but no one uses them any more. Let's start at this end and work our way down."

They began racing from one hut to the
next, flinging open the doors and peering in
through the windows.

But each one they came to was empty.

"Nothing, nothing, nothing!" stormed Puck, as he kicked his way out of the last hut. "Where can she be? And what's going to happen if we don't find Rosabel before Shadow's deadline?"

"I don't know, Puck," Holly replied, anxiously shaking her head. "But we're not going to be able to help Rosabel if we're exhausted. Let's find something to eat to keep us going."

"Good idea," Puck replied. "We'll go to the Lake of Gilded Lilies. It's not far from here and it's surrounded by amazing fruit trees. We can have glitterberries and stardrops and moonberries…"

Spurred on by the thought of food to revive

him, Puck flew swiftly to the lake. He
dropped down into a woody glade a little
way from the water's edge, where they
quickly picked the shining fruit.

"Delicious," sighed
Holly, resting against a
tree trunk for a
moment, as she
popped stardrops
into her mouth.

As Puck ate a mouthful of moonberries,
Holly stared through the long grasses toward
the lake. Its calm, clear waters shone crystal
blue in the afternoon sun, and Holly saw that

its surface was covered with giant lily pads, their creamy white flowers rimmed with gold…

"Puck!" she hissed suddenly, crouching down low and pulling Puck down with her. "Look! Over there – on that lily pad. I think it's Princess Rosabel!"

Chapter Five

"It is!" gasped Puck. "We've found the
princess at last. I'd recognize that dazzling
cloak anywhere! And there's Shadow
with her."

Both Puck and Holly silently took in the
scene: the little princess lay motionless on
the lily pad, the menacing figure of Shadow
towering over her.

Then, from the Dark Forest on the other
side of the lake, two huge ponies emerged,
their wings raised threateningly.

"Storm and Ravenstar," said Puck grimly.
"Shadow's helpers."

Shadow flew across the lake to meet them,

then all three ponies bent their heads in conversation.

"If only we knew what they were saying," said Holly.

"Shh!" said Puck. "I can just hear their voices carrying across the water."

He pricked his ears and waited. A moment later, Shadow was off, flying above the Dark Forest, his dark tail streaming behind him, while Storm and Ravenstar flew over and settled on the bank of the lake closest to Rosabel.

"What did they say?" whispered Holly.

"Storm and Ravenstar said they'd spied on the Spell-Keepers after they read Shadow's message, and that they're out looking for them. Then Shadow said something about making sure they don't get too close. It looks like he's left Storm and Ravenstar to guard Rosabel."

"Well now's our chance," said Holly. "We have to rescue Rosabel while Shadow's away."

"Then we need a plan," said Puck. "And fast! Maybe one of us should distract Storm and Ravenstar, while the other rescues Princess Rosabel?"

"We could try…" said Holly, sounding unsure. "But it's so risky. What happens if they don't fall for it? Aren't there any spells you can do?"

"Holly!" said Puck. "You know what my spells are like. They're hopeless! I can't even remember the spell for washing my hoofs. And I'd need a really powerful one to stop

Storm and Ravenstar."

"Then maybe we should sneak away and find the Spell-Keepers?" said Holly.

Puck's face fell. "But Shadow might come back and move Princess Rosabel before we can get help. We're so close now, there must be something we can do..." He stopped for a moment, looking across the lake lost in thought. "I've got it!" he cried suddenly. "A sleeping spell! I'll send Storm and Ravenstar to sleep. When my friend Dandelion did it on me, I slept for a whole afternoon."

"Brilliant!" said Holly. "Are you sure you know how it goes?"

"I'm sure," said Puck, nodding. "Let's creep through the long grass toward them. As soon as we're near enough, I'll say the spell."

Crouching as low as they could, Puck and Holly began to move toward the pony guards. Holly could see the tops of the grasses rustling, and could only hope it would look like the wind. As they neared Storm and Ravenstar, the two ponies seemed to loom bigger than

ever against the afternoon sky.

"I think we're close enough now," said
Puck. Holly stayed as still as she could, while
Puck began to say the words of the spell in a
hushed, soothing, sing-song voice:

"Quiet now and shut your eyes
Let nothing wake you, or make you rise
Fall into a trance-like sleep
Dream long, dream well, dream deep..."

To Holly's amazement, the two ponies' eyes
took on a glazed look. They slowly bent their
legs, their eyes closing almost as soon as their
knees touched the ground. Within seconds,
Storm and Ravenstar were snoring gently,
snuggled up beside each other.

"That was brilliant, Puck!" cried Holly climbing on to his back.

"It was, wasn't it?" cried Puck, equally

amazed. "I don't think any of my spells has ever worked so well."

Puck seemed to forget for a moment that they now had to save Rosabel, as he stood staring at the two sleeping ponies, a look of pride on his face.

"How long does the spell last?" asked Holly.

"Oh no," said Puck, his face falling. "I totally forgot that part. I should have said, *Sleep for hours, three or more, Take your slumbers by the shore...* They could wake up at any moment!"

"Then we've no time to lose – come on!" said Holly.

As they flew across the lake, Holly kept glancing back to keep an anxious eye on

Storm and Ravenstar.

"At last!" said Puck, as they touched down beside Rosabel, who was lying still and silent on the lily pad, the cloak draped around her.

"Princess Rosabel," said Holly, whispering in her ear. "We've come to rescue you."

But the princess stayed stock-still.

"Oh no!" said Puck. "You were right – she *is* under some kind of enchantment. Now what are we going to do?"

Chapter Six

Holly looked toward the shore for Storm and Ravenstar. They were still sleeping, but she was terrified at the thought of them waking suddenly. "We have to break the enchantment, or we'll never get her off the lily pad. Do you know any enchantment-breaking spells?"

Puck shook his head. "I don't," he said. "We'll have to think of another way to move her. Maybe we could carry her?"

"She's too heavy," said Holly, as she tried lifting one of Rosabel's front legs. "What about trying to move the lily pad? Maybe we could use it as a raft."

As she spoke, Holly bent over the water and began paddling with her hands, and Puck quickly followed suit with his hoofs.

"It won't move," said Puck. "Its roots are holding it fast."

"I know!" Holly cried. "The cloak! That's what has put her under the enchantment. Remember how her eyes became hard and glittery when she put it on? It must have been working its magic over her while we were making our costumes."

"Of course!" said Puck, his eyes lighting up. He gripped the cloak in his teeth and pulled it off, before flinging it into the water.

Rosabel got up with a start, blinking as if dazzled by the sunlight.

"Where am I?" she cried, sounding scared and unsure.

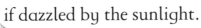

"Hush," said Holly gently. "You've been kidnapped by an evil pony named Shadow. The cloak is magic – it had you under a spell and brought you straight to him. We have to get you out of here before his guards wake up."

"This is all your fault!" huffed Princess Rosabel. "You two were supposed to be looking after me."

"What?" cried Puck. "After all we've done for you—"

"The important thing is that we need to leave," interrupted Holly. "Shadow's henchmen could wake at any moment. Follow us – we're going to fly straight to the Summer Palace."

Princess Rosabel leaped forward, stretching

out her wings, but then teetered at the edge of the lily pad, as if she was about to fall straight into the water. She flung herself backwards, landing in a heap on her bottom, her legs splayed out beneath her.

"I don't understand," she said, her voice filled with distress.

"My wings…they won't work. I can't fly!"

Holly looked at her anxiously.

"Oh no," said Puck. "Shadow must have put a spell on your wings to make sure you couldn't escape. Don't worry – the Pony

Queen will be able to undo it,
as soon as we get you back to the palace.
We'll just have to swim across the lake."

"I'm not swimming in that disgusting water," snapped Princess Rosabel. "It'll ruin my hair. You'll have to come up with a better plan than that."

"There isn't another plan," Puck replied stiffly. "And if we don't get out of here soon, they'll catch us for sure." He glanced nervously at the sleeping guards on the shore.

"It's too cold," said Princess Rosabel, dipping her hoof in. "I'll freeze in that water."

"Well, if that's how you feel…" said Puck, and he came up behind her, pushing her toward the water, "…I'll just have to help you in."

"Stop!" screamed Rosabel, as she reached the edge of the lily pad. "I can't...I can't swim."

Princess Rosabel was trembling. Holly tried to comfort her, putting her arms around her neck.

"You can't swim?" said Puck disbelievingly. "What about all those golden beaches you were boasting about? Haven't you ever been in the water?"

"My parents always said I was too precious

to risk it," sniffed Rosabel.

Puck looked exasperated. "Okay," he said. "That doesn't leave us with much choice. We'll just have to leave you here and go and get the Spell-Keepers."

"You're not leaving me!" wailed Princess Rosabel. "You can't!"

Holly scanned the lake, trying to find a way across, but she couldn't see anything except a group of turtles, their huge domed shells poking up above the surface of the water.

"Wait!" cried Holly suddenly. "I have an idea."

She grabbed Princess Rosabel's tiara, then held it out to the largest turtle, twisting it this way and that so that it sparkled in the sunlight.

"What are you doing?" demanded Rosabel. "That's mine."

"I know," Holly said calmly, taking care not to alarm the turtle, who was still swimming toward her, "but it could be our only way out of here. I've read that turtles like shiny things." When the turtle reached her hand she offered him the tiara, then mimed stepping onto his back, pointing in the direction of the lakeshore. The turtle nodded in understanding. Taking the tiara in his beak, he turned to the rest of his family, gesturing to them with his flippers. One by one the turtles lined up with their shells above the surface, forming a path across the water to the other side of the lake.

"Wow!" breathed Puck in admiration.

Holly turned to check on Rosabel and saw that she was terrified at the prospect of walking across the turtles' backs.

"You go first, Princess Rosabel," Puck suggested, "then Holly and I can come behind you." As he spoke, he gently pushed the princess from the lily pad onto the back of the first turtle, then smiled reassuringly back at Holly.

"I suppose if I have to do it…" Rosabel muttered, and quickly set off.

They made their way across the lake, stepping carefully from one turtle to the next, Holly making sure to thank each one as they went. *We're going to make it,* she thought to herself. *We're actually going to make it.*

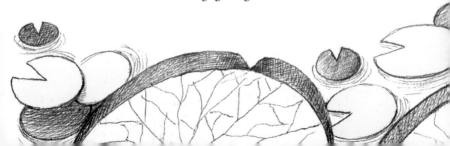

But a gasp from Puck made her look up.

"Oh no!" cried Rosabel.

There were Storm and Ravenstar, wide awake, waiting for them on the other side of the lake. "I still can't fly," cried Rosabel. "There's no escape."

"We've fought off Storm and Ravenstar before," said Puck determinedly. "We can do it again."

But even before he'd finished speaking, a dark shape flew over the forest and landed beside the lake. It was Shadow, his eyes filled with anger. "How dare you let Rosabel escape!" he said to his henchmen.

A moment later, all three ponies took to the air. "What should we do?" said Holly. "They're heading straight for us!"

Chapter Seven

In a panic, Princess Rosabel leaped off the last turtle and raced ahead of them…into the Dark Forest.

"Come back!" cried Puck. He turned to Holly. "We have to go after her this time."

Holly leaped onto Puck's back, but just as they tried to dive between the trees, Holly felt a sharp tug at her sleeve. To her horror, she saw Ravenstar snatching at her top, pulling her back. She grabbed onto Puck's mane to stop herself from falling. "Help!" she cried. "I've been caught."

Puck skidded to a halt as, with a soft thud, Shadow landed on their other side.

"The Pony Queen's little helpers," he said mockingly, towering over them. "I think it's time we taught you two a lesson."

Shadow and Storm moved closer still, until they formed a tight ring around Puck and Holly.

"So what should we do with them, Shadow?" asked Storm. "Hold them for ransom instead of the princess?"

"Don't think I've forgiven you two for falling asleep," Shadow snarled at his henchmen. "I still want to capture Rosabel. But, I doubt she's going to find her own way out of the Dark Forest. And in the meantime, I can think of a few little spells to cast over Puck and Holly here." He began to laugh nastily. "What shall we do? Take away

Puck's wings? Turn Holly to ice?"

Holly trembled at the spite in Shadow's voice.

"Not so fast!" came a shrill voice from the shadows.

Holly gasped as she saw Princess Rosabel appear on the path in front of them.

The little pony cantered toward them, chanting a spell beneath her breath:

"Clouds of cotton candy, sticky and sweet,
Wrap yourself around Shadow's feet.
Showers of sparkles, lilac and pink,
Fill the air and make them blink.
Princess perfume, smelling of flowers,
Fill this lake with your scented powers."

As the spell worked its magic, sparkly fireworks fizzed and popped around Shadow and his henchmen, forcing them to shut their eyes against the bright light.

Cotton candy clouds swirled around
Shadow's feet, sticking like glue to his hoofs as
he squirmed and kicked. And as the sickly,
overpowering scent of flowers filled the air,
Storm and Ravenstar began sneezing and
spluttering. Ravenstar let go of Holly as he
tried to shake free of the smell.

"Quick!" said Puck. "Come with me."

They galloped away as fast as they could,
taking the path around the lake.

"This way!" cried Puck, branching to the
right. "We can follow the river back to the
palace."

Chapter Eight

"I can't believe you came back for us," said Holly, as Princess Rosabel drew alongside her and Puck. "That was so brave of you."

"Well, I knew you two would never outwit Shadow," said Rosabel, her tone as haughty as ever.

Holly looked over at the little pony beside her, but Rosabel refused to meet her eye.

Holly guessed the princess must have been grateful or she would never have come back for them – she was just too proud to say so.

"Well, thank you!" said Holly, but Puck only snorted indignantly.

"We've gotten away from Shadow before," he said. "We could have done it again."

"Never mind that now," cried Holly. "Look! I think I can see the turrets of the Summer Palace."

"And the Pony Queen!" Puck added. She was flying along the river, a band of Spell-Keepers at her side. Then she fluttered down in a blaze of glittering sparkles, landing gracefully on the ground in front of them.

"Puck! Holly! Is it really you?" cried Bluebell, rushing forward. "We followed the

fireworks we saw in the sky. But what are you
doing here? And Princess Rosabel! I'm so glad
we've found you."

"What happened?" asked the Pony Queen.

"Shadow, Storm and Ravenstar are just there," said Puck, pointing back the way they'd come.

The Pony Queen looked to her Spell-Keepers. "Firefly! Snowdrop!" she said. "Go quickly! See if you can find them."

As Firefly and Snowdrop flew away, Puck began telling the Pony Queen how he and Holly had found Princess Rosabel on the lake and tried to rescue her, only for Shadow and his henchmen to come after them.

"So much for your promise," Bluebell pointed out.

"I'm sorry," said Puck, looking over at his mother. "I know you told us to stay out of trouble, but we had to try to help."

"It's all right," said Bluebell, nuzzling close to him. "I understand. I think you've been incredibly brave. I'm just relieved Shadow didn't hurt you."

There was a faint coughing sound as Rosabel cleared her throat. "Excuse me," she said. "But I was the one who saved everybody. Shadow was about to zap Puck and Holly to pieces when I came back for them and cast an amazing sparkly spell. Without me, they would have been toast."

Puck opened his mouth to protest, but the Pony Queen interrupted him. "Well, I think you've all acted courageously," she said gently.

As she spoke, Firefly and Snowdrop returned, their flanks heaving from flying so fast. "There's no sign of Shadow, Your Majesty, or Storm and Ravenstar. They must have heard us coming and made their escape."

"There's nothing else we can do now," said the Pony Queen. "Besides, we have other things to look forward to. I think we should all go back to the palace for a rest before this evening's Costume Contest."

"But, Your Majesty," said Snowdrop, "I thought you'd canceled it?"

"I had, but now Princess Rosabel has been found, and everyone is safe, I think we deserve a celebration."

She went over to the princess and breathed gently over her wings. "There," she said.

"That should restore your power of flight." And, smiling, she placed a new gleaming tiara on the princess's head.

Princess Rosabel tentatively flapped her wings and found she rose effortlessly from the ground. "Thank you, Your Majesty," she said graciously.

"I haven't heard Rosabel thanking us," Puck commented to Holly, as they flew back to the palace.

Holly giggled. Behind them, she could hear the princess chatting away with the Spell-Keepers.

"Of course I've had a very traumatic time," Rosabel was saying. "But naturally I'll come to the Costume Contest. I don't want to disappoint my fans. There must be lots of fairy ponies coming just to meet me."

Holly looked anxiously at Puck in case he was about to disagree, but this time he just caught Holly's eye and grinned.

"I know," he whispered to her. "She did come back for us. Even if she's a pain, she was there when it mattered most."

The Costume Contest began as the sun set over Butterfly Valley, streaking the sky with a rose-tinted glow. Puck and Holly gazed around them as the fairy ponies pranced among the flowers in their amazing costumes. Some were adorned with garlands, others had threaded petals through their manes and tails and one had a butterfly cloak that shimmered and danced as she moved, the butterflies rising and falling from her body in waves.

"Look at her," said Puck, pointing to a fairy pony surrounded by a cloud of sparkles that coated her all the way from the tip of her nose to her glittering hoofs.

"I don't know how the Pony Queen will ever choose a winner," said Holly, her voice filled with wonder.

"It would have been easy," said Princess Rosabel, joining them. "If I still had my cloak

I'd definitely have won. It's all your fault I don't have a costume, Puck. After all, you did throw it in the water."

"But it was enchanted!" Puck protested.

"That's not the point," said Princess Rosabel. "And you, Holly, gave my most precious tiara to that turtle," she huffed.

At that moment a tinkling bell sounded, and all the fairy ponies lined up, ready for the judging to begin. The Pony Queen came trotting over to them.

"I'd like to reward you all for your bravery today," she said. "Would you like to help me judge the contest?"

"Oh! Yes please!" Holly and Puck cried together.

"I'll hand the prize to the winner though,"

said Rosabel, as they followed the Pony Queen to the judging stands. "After all, I am her special guest."

Puck just rolled his eyes this time. Nothing was going to take away from his enjoyment of the contest.

"You two come with me," said the Pony Queen to Puck and Holly. "We'll walk along the Costume Parade together. When you see the pony you want to win, you're to twitch your tail three times."

"What about me?" asked Holly, slightly forlornly.

"Ah yes, of course," said the Pony Queen, smiling. "You can touch Puck's mane. Now remember, you're looking for a costume that is both inventive and beautiful."

Holly was sure she'd never be able to choose the one she liked the most. She was torn between a pony dressed almost entirely in flowers, with a train of leaves that rustled in her wake, and a River Pony who wore a seaweed cloak decorated with shining jewels and delicate curling shells.

Then, as they walked along the line, Holly, Puck and the Pony Queen all gasped together. There was a pony in a costume so light and delicate it seemed to dance on the wind. It was made entirely from cobwebs, each strand like spun silver, sparkling with dewdrops.

Holly and Puck made their secret signs and turned back to whisper the winner in Rosabel's ear.

Princess Rosabel simpered and smirked as she handed out the prize to a young pony named Tulip. All the ponies stamped their hoofs in applause, as Tulip stood on the dais to show off her amazing costume. Then the Pony Queen stepped forward.

"I have a special announcement to make," she began. "As most of you know, Shadow has once again tried to claim my crown for himself today, by kidnapping Princess Rosabel. But with the princess's courage and quick thinking, Shadow has once again been thwarted. Please thank Puck and Holly, too, for their role in saving the princess."

"Three cheers for Princess Rosabel!" shouted the crowd. "And three cheers for Puck and Holly!"

While Rosabel basked in the cheers from the crowd, a delighted smile on her face, Puck and Holly looked at the ground and blushed,

hiding themselves away as soon as they could.

But it wasn't long before Bluebell sought them out, her face wreathed in smiles. A fairy pony they hadn't met before was standing by her side. His coat was a soft brown, his wings radiant and regal.

"This is Amaranth, from Waterfall Island," Bluebell said. "He's heard what you two did for Princess Rosabel."

"Indeed I have," said Amaranth gravely. "And I know Princess Rosabel's parents would like to reward you. So, on their behalf, I am inviting you to Waterfall Island for Princess Rosabel's birthday celebrations, which will take place this winter."

For a moment, Puck and Holly were too stunned to speak. Puck quickly looked over at

Holly, widening his eyes to show his horror.
Holly looked down before she started to
laugh.

"A trip to Waterfall Island with Princess
Rosabel," said Bluebell. "Isn't that
wonderful?"

"It is – thank you!" said Holly,
remembering her manners. "Thank you very
much."

"Yes – um – thank you," Puck added.
"That's very kind."

Bluebell looked slightly puzzled by their
reaction, but before she could say more,
another fairy pony came up, asking to be
introduced to Amaranth.

"What an honor!" said Bluebell.

Holly started giggling.

"I can't believe it," Puck groaned. "*More* Princess Rosabel. She is the most spoiled, infuriating…"

"She did seem a little spoiled," admitted Bluebell. "I can see that might not have been the best reward for both of you. Maybe we had better go home for some blueberry fizzle cakes as an extra treat…"

"And toffee apples?" pleaded Puck.

"And toffee apples," Bluebell agreed.

As they took to the skies, Holly wrapped her arms around Puck's neck.

"We make a good team, don't we?" said Puck. "We've defeated Shadow again *and*

managed to survive Princess Rosabel. Promise me you'll come back for more adventures?"

"I promise," said Holly. "Who knows what tricks Shadow might try next time…"

Enter the world of the

Fairy Ponies

and collect every enchanting tale

For more Fairy Ponies titles
visit our website at

www.edcpub.com or
www.usbornebooksandmore.com